Josie
the
Singing Butterfly
Volume 4 / Adventures #15-18

Josie Waverly
Illustrations by Frances Espanol

Print information available on the last page.

Rev. date: 07/05/2018

To order additional copies of this book, contact:
Xlibris
1-888-795-4274
www.Xlibris.com
Orders@Xlibris.com

JOSIE WAVERLY

Illustrations by:
Frances Espanol

"JOSIE SAVES SLIPPERY SNAKE"

On a brisk fall day. When it was cool outside.
Slippery snake slipped into a leaf pile to hide.
Josie the Singing Butterfly
thought to herself,
"Hmmm, now what was that about?"
Then she flew down closer to the pile
so she could check it out.

"Slippery?" called Josie.
"Why are you in there?"
Slippery hissed as he told Josie,
"I have no one to care.
No one likes me.
They say I'm too scary.
Because I'm not pretty like a princess fairy."

4

Josie said, "Oh Slippery that's not true!
Yes, you might be gray and scaly
but I'm not afraid of you.
Now come on out and we'll have fun
singing a sing a song or two."
Soon Slippery slithered out
and he sang with all his pride.
With Josie as his friend
he didn't feel like he had to hide.
"No more hiding Slippery", said Josie.
"Not this day, not any! You will make more
friends in time. Yes many, many, many!"

6

JOSIE'S LESSON:

True beauty starts on the inside.

"JOSIE & BILLY BEAVER"

Billy Beaver was running down the edge
of the creek at a super-fast pace.
When he stumbled over a rock
and landed on his face.
Flying overhead, Josie the Singing Butterfly
saw him take his nasty stumble.
She flew down beside him, and while he got up,
she heard him start to mumble.

Still stunned, Billy said,
"Josie, I think I knocked my tooth loose
when I hit that rock."
Josie said, "WOW I guess you did,
with her face showing her shock."
She said "The one in front, there on the left,
is sticking out and really loose right now.
We need to get you to Dentist Barney
Beaver, so he can fix it somehow."

"Come one Billy. I will sing you a song
while we walk to Dentist Barney."
Billy replied, "Josie I am really scared
will you stay right here beside me?"
"Of course I will!" said Josie,
"and don't worry you'll be fine.
Tooth or no tooth, you'll always
be a furry friend of mine."

11

JOSIE LESSON:

Comfort your friend who might be afraid.

"JOSIE & DODGER DOG DAYS"

Outside on the cabin porch,
one warm summer day, there he laid
stretched out in a lazy "dog-day" sort of way.
Dodger dog was laying on his favorite seat.
By his side a bowl of water and a bone to eat.
When Josie the Singing Butterfly
came to visit, fluttering towards the ground.
She landed right on Dodger's head
and her brightly colored wings
stood out against his fur so brown.

He said, "Hey there Josie 'ol gal
what brings you here today?"
Josie asked, "Dodger, my buddy,
why are you resting
and not up ready to play?"
"READY TO PLAY?"
a question Dodger loudly fired.
"I have run and jumped
all morning Josie.
I am totally tired!"
It's time for a rest now, even
you must know, none of us
can constantly go, go, go."

16

Dodger said, "Josie, your wings need
some rest to get strong again,
or they won't work as good
as they have been.
And your brain needs to sleep
to grow big and strong,
so tomorrow you can be ready
to sing a new song."

17

Josie listened for a while,
as Dodger talked on.
Taking each of his words to heart.
When he was done she agreed
it had been a long day from the start.
She told him good bye
and shouted one last reminder
as she flew on her merry way.
"Rest for now Dodger. My buddy. My friend.
I will return another day."

JOSIE LESSON:

Know when to work hard
and when to take a rest.
Listen to your body!

"JOSIE MEETS KATIE CAT"

Flying high in the sky gives
Josie the Singing Butterfly
so much more to see.
Houses, cars, and people.
A ragged worn tire swing
tied in an old oak tree.
Down by the tree Josie spots
something she's never seen before,
while asking herself "What's that?"
As she flies closer it looks like
something the others warned her about.
A little black and white cat.

21

The little cat swats and swats at Josie.
Then chases her around and around.
Josie thinks the little cat is playing
so, she flies down closer to the ground.
Suddenly the little cat pounced at
Josie. Almost knocking her out!
Josie yelled, "Hey wait a minute little
cat! What's this all about?"

The little cat said bluntly,
"I'm a frisky little cat and this is what I do!
By the way I'm called Katie Cat,
and just who the heck are you?"
She answered, "I'm Josie, and I'm a singing
butterfly that likes to make new friends
but after you hit me to the ground
this is where my visit ends!"

Katie Cat said "Aw Josie please don't fly away. Forgive me for what I've done.
I'm sorry I did that to you. I'll try to be more
careful next time we're having fun."
Josie forgave Katie Cat and for hours they
continued to play by the old tree swing.
Becoming friends with Katie Cat gave
Josie's heart a more joyful song to sing!

JOSIE LESSON:

We all need to practice forgiveness and compassion towards others.

Printed in the United States
By Bookmasters